Lisa loves to cause trouble. . . .

"Poor Dandy! Wasted on a major chicken!" Lisa Harris said in a nasty tone.

"What is that supposed to mean?" Jessie said. "Pam is not a chicken!"

"Oh, yeah? That shows what you know!" said Lisa. "She doesn't deserve Dandy. She's scared to death of horses. And she hates it here. She wouldn't even be at pony camp if you weren't so pushy. *You* forced her to come!"

"Says who?" Jessie asked angrily.

"Says her!" said Lisa, pointing at me. "She told Sally last night. Just ask her!"

"Well, Pam?" said Jessie, her eyes narrowed as she looked at me.

"Jessie, I didn't say that!" I yelped. "All I said was that I—"

"Thanks a lot!" Jessie cried. "Feel free to stop coming here anytime!"

Jessie stamped away.

Don't miss any of the books in
this fabulous new series!

And look for this other great series
from HarperPaperbacks:

*Ballet
School*

PONY CAMP

Pam's Trail Ride Adventure

SUSAN SAUNDERS

HarperPaperbacks
A Division of HarperCollins*Publishers*

HarperPaperbacks *A Division of* HarperCollins*Publishers*
10 East 53rd Street, New York, N.Y. 10022

Copyright © 1994 by Susan Saunders and
Daniel Weiss Associates, Inc.
Cover art copyright © 1994 Daniel Weiss Associates, Inc.

Produced by Daniel Weiss Associates, Inc.,
33 West 17th Street, New York, New York 10011.

First printing: July 1994

Printed in the United States of America

HarperPaperbacks and colophon are trademarks of
HarperCollins*Publishers*

10 9 8 7 6 5 4 3 2

Pam's Trail Ride Adventure

How did I ever end up at pony camp? I asked myself for the millionth time as my dad's car pulled into the driveway of Horizon Hills Farm. Every morning, I thought the same thing—how did someone like me end up in a place with so many gigantic animals?

My name is Pam Werner. I think I must have been scared by something big and furry when I was a baby. *Something* must have happened, because I really don't like getting within a hundred feet of any animal larger than my cat, Stanley.

I don't like a lot of change, either.

I've lived in the same house and gone to the same school forever. And the most important thing of all is that I've always had the same best friend. That's how I wound up at pony camp. When Jessie Johnson asked me to go with her to Horizon Hills Farm, I said I would give it a try. After all, we've done everything together since we were babies.

Horizon Hills Farm is where kids go to learn horseback riding. It's not *just* riding—there's swimming, and baseball, and crafts. Basically, though, you go to Horizon Hills to learn about horses. And that means that every morning you climb onto an animal about the size of a truck!

Sure, I could have said no to Jessie. I could have gone back to Camp Ogunquit, the day camp where we've spent all our summers from kindergarten to third grade.

But I knew how important pony camp was to Jessie. She's been asking for a horse of her own since she could talk. So she was positive that pony camp would be terrific. Jessie never stopped talking about how we would jump tall fences and go on major trail rides in no time at all.

As soon as I told Jessie I would go to pony camp with her, I had a nightmare. I was riding a huge horse down a trail. Suddenly the horse started to run. It ran faster . . . and faster . . . until trees and rocks were just blurs flashing past.

I tugged on the reins in my hands. But the horse ignored me. I could tell he didn't want to stop until we had raced across the entire country, and right into the Pacific Ocean! Or until I fell off. And suddenly I *was* falling. I woke up with a jerk. I had fallen out of bed.

This was not a good sign. But I couldn't tell my parents about my nightmare trail ride—they'd never let me go to pony camp.

And I definitely couldn't tell Jessie.

I know I should be able to tell my best friend everything. But to Jessie, a pen full of horses is no scarier than a basket full of kittens. She would think I was a total wimp.

I wished more than anything that I was heading back to safe old Camp Ogunquit. But could I spend two whole summer months without my best friend?

No way.

Besides, there was one really cool thing about pony camp. I would need lots of new clothes! Riding clothes are great—stretch jeans with leather knee patches, U.S. Equestrian Team T-shirts, riding tights, knee boots, even riding *sneakers*.

I ended up with three pairs of jeans, two blue and one black, a denim shirt with silver buttons, and some short leather boots. I also found a neat riding hat—navy blue with white stars. My dad even got me a T-shirt that said I'D RATHER BE RIDING. But I was pretty certain that I *wouldn't*.

The first few weeks of pony camp were actually pretty fun. At Horizon Hills Farm, you keep the same horse for the entire summer. Right from the start I knew my horse, Gracie, was perfect for me.

Gracie likes cats as much as I do. She shares her stall with four of them—Jane the barn cat and Jane's three kittens.

Gracie is a chestnut—her shade is a caramel color—with a white streak down her face and two white feet. She's very pretty. Better than that, she's very calm.

Horses are not all alike. Some are naturally more trouble than others. Like Ranger, Jessie's horse. In the beginning, Jessie and Ranger had lots of problems. He liked to stop short, so that Jessie shot out of the saddle and ended up on his neck. Once, Jessie actually fell all the way off! She hit the ground so hard that she couldn't breathe for a second.

Ranger gave her a really hard time, until Jessie figured out what she should be doing.

But Gracie wasn't like that. Gracie gave me plenty of time to catch on.

She was always patient. She never made

any sudden moves. She was slow and steady.

It's a good thing Jessie didn't get Gracie. She'd be bored by how calm Gracie is.

But calm is just fine with me. I don't like surprises from big, furry animals.

Diana Kirk says the most important thing to remember about riding is to stay relaxed. But how can you be relaxed on a wild and crazy horse like Ranger? I don't know how Jessie does it.

The campers at Horizon Hills are divided into groups of beginning riders and groups of intermediate riders. Diana is the riding instructor of our beginners group.

There are four of us in the group. There's me and Jessie. Then there's Maxine Brown. We know her from Westbrook Elementary School—she's going to be in the fourth grade this fall, just like us. Diana says Maxine is a natural rider. But Maxine isn't a show-off about it.

The fourth kid in our group is Peter

Brody. He's a fifth grader from Jamestown, the next town over.

Peter is a little chubby. His parents thought riding would be a good way for him to get some exercise. But he didn't really want to go to Horizon Hills, so he grumbles sometimes.

We did a lot in the first two weeks of camp. I learned how to groom Gracie and how to bridle and saddle her.

After two weeks I could walk Gracie, and steer, and back her up. I could even do a sitting trot—a trot is one notch faster than a walk.

I was amazed by how quickly I was catching on. But I knew most of the credit went to Gracie. If Gracie weren't so easy-going, I would have been too nervous to learn anything!

We were just beginning to post. Posting means raising yourself out of the saddle as your horse trots instead of just sitting there, bouncing around like a bag of potatoes like I do.

7

You count "Ah-one" while you're lifting yourself up. And then "Ah-two" while you're lowering yourself back down. And you miss one of the horse's bounces.

The morning after we started posting, Jessie was complaining as Dad drove us to Horizon Hills. It was weird to hear Jessie groaning about going to pony camp—usually I just looked out the window and wondered why *I* was going.

"My legs are *so* sore!" she said when we stopped at the barn. "It feels like I ran twenty miles yesterday instead of just posting on Ranger for half an hour!"

"Ranger must be kind of rough," I told her. "Gracie's trot is like sitting in a swing."

I wasn't sore at all. I was actually looking forward to practicing my posting again!

"Bye, Dad," Jessie called, climbing out of the car.

"Pam's mom will pick you up this afternoon," Mr. Johnson told us. "Have fun."

"Look, Pam! There are Peter and

Maxine," Jessie said as her dad drove away. "I wonder what's up."

All the campers usually go straight into the barn to see their horses. But that morning, Peter and Maxine were hanging out at the side door of the barn.

Maxine is small and blond and super-neat. I like Maxine, but I always feel like a total slob next to her. I don't know how she manages to keep all the dirt off her riding boots!

Peter is just the opposite. His shirt always hangs out of his pants, and all his clothes are always totally wrinkled. He's usually munching something sticky.

That morning, Peter wasn't eating anything. Both he and Maxine looked really serious. And they seemed to be waiting for me and Jessie.

As soon as they spotted us they started talking in low voices. "What's going on?" I called when Jessie and I were close enough.

Peter and Maxine glanced at each other.

"It's . . . uh . . . Gracie," Peter said.

"Gracie?" I asked, suddenly feeling sick.

Horses are big, but they're not as strong as you might think. Diana had told us about a horse at the stable who died of a stomachache!

"Is she . . ." I began, fearing the worst.

"She's basically okay," Maxine said quickly.

"She pulled a muscle in her leg," Peter explained. "Diana says it's not too—"

But I didn't wait to hear any more. I was already racing into the barn. Jessie, Maxine, and Peter were right behind me.

2

I hurried up the alley—that's the long hall that runs down the center of the barn. Stalls for the horses line it on both sides. The alley was full of kids in boots and riding hats, the way it is every morning.

The stalls for our four horses are right in a row. Diana always waits for us there.

But I didn't see Diana anywhere. And Gracie's stall door was hanging open.

I skidded to a stop before I reached it. I didn't want to scare Gracie by bursting in on her. And I also didn't want to scare *myself*—I was afraid of seeing Gracie really sick.

Then Diana stuck her head out of Gracie's stall. "Pam? Come on in. The veterinarian has already checked Gracie out. He says she'll be fine."

"What happened to her?" I asked, trying to catch my breath.

"We're not sure," said Diana. "Yesterday we turned a few of the horses into the field to give them some fresh air. Gracie bruised her leg somehow, running and playing. It happens."

I followed Diana into Gracie's stall.

Jane the barn cat was there, as usual. She and her three kittens were asleep on a bale of hay in the corner.

Gracie whinnied softly when she saw me. She stuck her neck out and nibbled at my sleeve, the way she always does.

I patted Gracie's nose as I looked her over. She was standing on three legs, holding her back left foot in the air.

"See the swelling just below her hock?" Diana asked.

Jessie, Maxine, and Peter had crowded in near the stall door.

"The hock is that big joint sticking out like an elbow," Jessie told us. She reads horse books the way other kids read comics.

An inch or two below Gracie's hock there was a lump the size of a tennis ball.

"Poor Gracie!" I said. "I bet that really hurts."

"How do you treat it?" Maxine asked Diana.

"For the first week we spray the swelling with cold water during the day. At night, we apply heat," Diana said. "Then next week we'll massage her leg with liniment. Liniment is a medicine that makes bruises heal more quickly."

"How quickly?" Peter asked. "How long will Gracie be crippled?"

I saw him stick his hand into his pocket. He slipped Gracie a sour ball. Peter can be grumpy sometimes, but basically he's a nice person.

"We hope not more than a couple of weeks," Diana said. She looked at me with concern.

"Don't worry about me," I said. "If you'll show me how, I can spend my mornings taking care of Gracie. Or just keeping her company."

After all, two weeks wasn't that long.

Diana smiled and shook her head. "You won't have to do that, Pam. I can take care of her leg."

"And Gracie has Jane and the kittens for company," Maxine added.

I looked back at Gracie. She was nosing the kittens around on the bale of hay. Sometimes she acts like she's their mother instead of Jane.

"Then what is Pam supposed to do?" Jessie asked Diana. "All the other horses belong to campers already."

We all nodded. Jessie had tried to switch Ranger for another horse the first week of camp. But the only horse available was a

14

tiny Shetland pony! So we knew that every horse was taken.

That was fine with me. As far as I was concerned, I was a one-horse rider. Gracie was the only horse I wasn't afraid of.

"I can learn a lot by watching you guys ride," I said. "I'll surprise Gracie with everything I know when she gets better."

Diana said, "You won't have to watch, Pam. Last weekend Mr. Morgan bought a new horse for the stable. I'm sure you're going to like him."

A new horse? Suddenly I felt so dizzy that I almost sat down on Jane and the kittens.

"Excellent, Pam!" Jessie said, slapping me on the shoulder. "You won't have to fall behind!"

Jessie is my best friend, but even best friends don't have exactly the same thoughts. Sometimes Jessie is so far from knowing my feelings that it makes me want to pinch her.

"Where is the new horse?" Peter and

15

Maxine asked at the same time.

"In the stall next to Mr. Morgan's office," Diana said. "Why don't we take a look at him?"

Everybody else was really excited. But my mind went blank on the way over to the owner's office. Why hadn't I pulled a muscle in *my* leg?

Then Diana was opening the stall door. Maxine looked inside and gasped.

"He's *beautiful!*" she cried.

"Wow!" said Peter. "Way cool!"

"He's like a movie horse!" said Jessie. "*King of the Mustangs*! Or that Arabian horse in *Always a Winner!*"

They were all right.

The horse was the color of coffee ice cream, with a vanilla mane and tail and a white diamond on his forehead. He had small, pointy ears, a wide face, big brown eyes, and dainty legs.

"Pam, this is Dandy. Jessie's right—he *is* an Arabian," Diana said with a nod.

"Arabians are a very old breed of horse. They are fast, and strong, and smart enough to be able to live in the desert."

"But we don't live in a desert," I mumbled. I couldn't get excited about this new horse.

This horse was nothing like Gracie.

Gracie stands in one place and blinks thoughtfully. The new horse paced back and forth, shaking his mane around.

He wasn't going to be sharing his stall with any cats, that was clear. He would step all over them!

The new horse twitched his ears and arched his neck. He was checking us out, and he was dancing around so that we'd check *him* out, too!

This horse was a show-off. He was all wrong for me. While the others were talking about how great he was, I was trying to think of a way out of this mess.

Suddenly a voice behind us said, "I know this horse! It's Dandy, isn't it?"

Lisa Harris was peering into the stall, along with her best friend, Sally Keller.

Lisa and Sally are intermediate riders. Lisa's brother, Kevin, is in their group, too, along with a boy named Bill Frano.

Lisa and Kevin think they know all there is to know about horses—and everything else.

Lisa is always nasty to Maxine. Diana says it's because Lisa is jealous that Maxine is such a good rider.

Kevin picks on Peter. They go to the same school, and Kevin is always teasing Peter about his weight.

And Kevin and Lisa both made fun of Jessie when she was having problems with Ranger.

So far, the Harrises had ignored me. I guess I wasn't worth bothering with.

"Yes, Lisa, it is Dandy," Diana said. She didn't seem too happy to see Lisa either.

"He belongs to Kathy Farrow. Right, Sally?" Lisa said.

Sally nodded. She hardly ever said anything.

Jessie and I were never sure whether Sally was too snobby to talk or whether she was just afraid she might say something wrong in front of Lisa.

"We saw Kathy ride him at a horse show a couple of weekends ago," Lisa went on.

I felt my stomach drop. Dandy was a show horse, too? I've watched show horses on TV. They always look jumpy and nervous.

"Yes, but Kathy was getting too tall for him," Diana said. "The Farrows bought Kathy a new horse and sold Dandy to Mr. Morgan."

"Really? Then I'll trade Rambo for him!" said Lisa.

Rambo is the big brown horse that Lisa rides at Horizon Hills.

"Like she's in charge here!" Maxine said under her breath.

"Yeah! In your dreams, Lisa," Peter added.

"Dandy is Pam's now!" Jessie said loudly.

"You have a horse, Lisa," said Diana. "Pam doesn't. Her horse pulled a leg muscle. So Pam will be riding Dandy, at least until Gracie recovers."

"Pam?" Lisa said, as though she couldn't imagine who Pam was.

She glanced around at the four of us. She gave Jessie a nasty look. Then she gave Maxine a nasty look. And then Peter. Finally, her eyes fell on me.

"*She's* going to ride Dandy?" Lisa sniffed.

Then Lisa and Sally looked at each other.

Sally shrugged.

"What a total waste of excellent horseflesh!" Lisa announced. Before anyone could speak, she marched off, Sally just a step behind her.

3

After my first day on Dandy, I completely agreed with Lisa. I was awful. I couldn't do anything right.

Jessie, Maxine, Peter, and I ride in one of the outdoor rings when the weather is nice. There's a tall white fence around it. We take turns doing our stuff while Diana watches and gives us tips.

About the third time that I dropped the reins that morning—or maybe it was the second time my feet slid out of the stirrups—I said to Diana, "I think Lisa Harris was right. I'm not a good enough rider for this horse. Why don't you let Lisa have him, and I'll wait for Gracie to get better?"

"Don't be silly," Diana said firmly. "I'll tell you what 'good' is. 'Good' is learning to saddle, and bridle, and walk, and steer, and sitting trot, and post in two weeks. And that's what you have done, Pam."

"But that was on *Gracie*," I said.

"It all works the same way on Dandy," Diana told me. "Remember, Pam, just relax. Peter, let me see your sitting trot, please."

While Peter was bumping around the ring, Maxine said, "Pam, if I had listened to Lisa, I would have given up riding after my first lesson. She's nasty to everybody."

"Maxine's right. Lisa loves to be mean!" Jessie said to me. "Especially if she doesn't get her way. You just have to ignore her, Pam."

It was nice to have such good friends. But I knew that Lisa Harris wasn't my biggest problem. My biggest problem was *me*. I didn't feel right. Not on Dandy.

He moved too fast!

It takes Gracie a while to build up speed from a walk to a trot. On Dandy, I barely squeezed my legs against his sides and he was practically galloping! It made me think of my trail ride nightmare.

Plus, Gracie and I are pals. Sometimes when we're standing in the ring, Gracie will turn her head around and nibble at the toe of my boot in a friendly way.

Not Dandy. Dandy was strictly business. He kept his eyes and ears pointed forward and shifted his feet. He could hardly wait for his turn to show off.

Whenever I messed up, he would shake his head until his ears flopped. He seemed to be saying, "Can't you do any better than that, bozo? When do I get a *real* rider?"

I never thought I would last until noon. But I did. I wobbled out of the barn toward the picnic tables where we eat our lunches.

"Those were the longest three hours of my life!" I said to Jessie, Maxine, and Peter.

The four of us sat down and unwrapped our sandwiches.

"But you got through it," Maxine pointed out. "And it will be easier tomorrow."

"You worry too much, Pam," Jessie put in. "Dandy is a neat horse!"

"It will take you a few days to get used to Dandy," Maxine said. "That's normal."

"He has to get used to you, too," Peter said. Peter and his horse, Hogan, had their ups and downs. "In the beginning, I bribed Hogan with sour balls."

"Maybe we won't need to get used to each other," I said. "Maybe Gracie's leg will heal quicker than the vet thought. Maybe I'll be riding her again by the end of the week."

But when Jessie and I stopped by Gracie's stall late that afternoon, she didn't look any better.

Jane was dozing on Gracie's broad back, the way she often does. But Gracie was still standing on three legs.

Jessie and I touched the lump below her

hock—it was hard, and hotter than the rest of her leg.

Gracie gave me a friendly nudge with her nose, and I rubbed her neck for a minute. I probably would have cried if I had been alone.

It looked like Dandy and I would be forced to get along, at least for a while.

"I guess we'd better hurry," I said to Jessie. "Mom has a meeting to go to tonight." My mom is a trustee of our library.

But when we stepped out of the barn, Mom wasn't tapping the steering wheel and looking at her watch like I thought she'd be. She wasn't even in the car. She was leaning against a white station wagon, talking to a man and a woman.

"Who is that?" Jessie asked me.

"I've never seen them before," I said. "But Mom seems to know them pretty well."

The three of them were talking a mile a minute and laughing a lot.

"This is my daughter, Pam," Mom said as

Jessie and I walked up to them. "And this is her friend Jessie Johnson. Girls, this is Mr. and Mrs. Keller. We haven't seen each other since college!"

"Keller?" Jessie and I said at the same time.

"That's right," Mrs. Keller said. "Maybe you know our daughter Sally."

Mrs. Keller had a nice smile and light-brown hair just like Sally's.

"I can't believe it," Jessie said in a low voice. "Your mom is friends with the *Kellers*!"

I couldn't believe it either.

"Here comes Sally now," said Mrs. Keller.

Jessie and I turned toward the barn.

Sally strolled through the side door—with Lisa Harris, of course. Lisa was jabbering at her, a frown on her face. Sally was just listening, as usual.

They didn't notice us until they were pretty close to the car. Then Lisa glanced up and gave the Kellers a big, fake smile. "Hi,

Mr. and Mrs. Keller!" she said brightly.

But Lisa looked puzzled. She was probably trying to figure out why Jessie and I were standing with the Kellers.

Sally smiled, too. It was an uncomfortable smile.

"Hello, Lisa. Sally, this is Mrs. Werner, Pam's mother. She and your dad and I went to college together!" Mrs. Keller said excitedly. "We haven't seen her in years. We had no idea we were living so close."

"Really?" Sally asked weakly. She kept looking over at Lisa, as if she was worried.

"And Mrs. Werner has solved our problem for tomorrow night," Mr. Keller said to Sally.

"My husband and I have to be out of town for two days," Mrs. Keller explained to me.

"Mrs. Werner has invited you to spend Wednesday night at her house," Mr. Keller told Sally. "Mr. Werner will pick you up here tomorrow afternoon."

"And you'll catch a ride to Horizon Hills with Jessie and Pam on Thursday morning," Mom added. "Mrs. Johnson will be driving you."

"Wow, Pam, that'll be great," Jessie muttered, just loud enough for me—and maybe Sally—to hear.

I felt like telling Jessie that this wasn't my fault, but I couldn't exactly do that!

"This way you won't have to miss any camp, Sally," Mrs. Keller said happily. "And we'll be back in time to get you on Thursday afternoon."

"I thought I could stay with Lis—" Sally began.

Mr. Keller didn't let her finish. "No, it's all settled, thanks to Mary Ann."

Maybe he thought Sally hung around with Lisa too much. I turned around to whisper this to Jessie, but she made a face and started toward the car.

Lisa looked mad, too.

And *I* was the one who had to have a

sleepover with the enemy!

Mom and the Kellers started talking again. Lisa snuck up next to me.

"Dandy is going to be my horse!" she said. "You can count on it!" She poked me with her elbow on her way into the Kellers' car.

I couldn't believe the day I was having. First Gracie's accident. Then getting stuck with Dandy. Then Sally Keller coming to spend the night.

Now Lisa was out to get me. And Jessie was mad, too. Where would it end?

4

Jessie sat in the backseat of our car with her lips pressed together all the way home. She didn't say one word. It wasn't fair!

But I didn't want to argue with her in front of my mom. So I kept my mouth shut.

As soon as we let Jessie out at her house, though, I yelled at Mom. "How could you do this to me? Sally Keller is awful!"

"What has she ever done to you?" Mom asked.

I thought really hard. I was sure I could convince Mom that Sally was too mean to sleep over. But no matter how much I thought about it, I couldn't come up with anything bad to say about Sally.

There were plenty of things to complain about with Lisa. But Sally wasn't Lisa, any more than I'm Jessie.

"That's what I thought," Mom said when I didn't answer her. "Sally's parents are both very nice people—I can't believe their child could be such a monster. At any rate, having her spend one night with us is not going to kill you!"

And that was that.

At least I had an excuse the next morning.

"You know how it is once my mom makes up her mind," I said to Jessie.

"Yeah. I guess you couldn't really say no," Jessie finally agreed.

"Not without getting into trouble," I said.

But I could tell that Sally's sleepover was still bothering Jessie. When we met Maxine in the barn, the first thing Jessie said was, "You'll never guess who is spending tonight at Pam's—not in a million years!"

"Who?" asked Maxine.

"Sally Keller!" Jessie said.

Maxine raised her eyebrows. "No way!"

"Way," said Jessie.

"Look," I complained, "it's not my fault."

But Jessie didn't answer me. And soon I had another thing to worry about.

The owner of Horizon Hills, Mr. Morgan, had turned a big bucket upside down in the middle of the alley. He climbed up on it and clapped his hands.

"Campers! May I have your attention?" he called in a loud voice.

All the kids stopped fiddling with their horses to listen.

"As you know, we have two trail rides a session at Horizon Hills," Mr. Morgan said. "You are all doing so well that we've decided to have our first ride next Tuesday!"

A trail ride? So far, I had only ridden in a fenced-in ring. Now I was supposed to ride Dandy in the wide-open spaces? All I could think of was my nightmare. What if Dandy ran away with me the way the nightmare horse had?

There was a lot of clapping and some whistling from the kids, but Mr. Morgan held up his hands for quiet.

"We'll make a day of it. We'll cut across the big field, ride through the woods, wade through a stream, and end up at the ocean," he said. "Then we'll have a cookout before we ride back."

All the kids cheered.

"I can't wait!" Jessie yelled, jumping up and down. "I've been looking forward to this for eight and a half years!"

She certainly wasn't going to understand what I was feeling.

Maxine looked a little worried—and she's a great rider. That made me feel better.

But then Maxine said, "I'm going to have to buy one of those little fly nets for Winnie's ears. And some bug spray. Do you think there are snakes in the woods?"

Maxine wasn't worried about the ride.

She was worried about the outdoors.

Peter was worried about the food. "I wonder what we'll get to eat at the cook-out," he said.

None of them were worried about controlling their horses. I tried to imagine Dandy and me on the trail. Dandy was galloping, full speed ahead, up and down hills, crashing through the forest, hopping over logs, thrashing across rivers . . .

Just like my nightmare trail ride!

5

"Maybe Gracie will heal quickly!" I said that to myself a zillion times, like a magic spell.

I had brought Gracie a whole apple and two carrots from home. I even had a plastic bag full of melon balls left over from dinner the night before.

"Gracie, these are full of vitamins and probably a lot of other good stuff, too," I told her. "If you eat every bite, you'll heal much faster."

But as Gracie gobbled everything down, I looked at the lump on her leg.

The lump certainly wasn't any smaller. In fact, I thought maybe it was larger. I was doomed!

I walked slowly to Dandy's stall. After thinking about my nightmare, I didn't even want to climb onto Dandy in the inside riding ring.

So I put it off as long as I could.

I groomed Dandy until Diana said, "Pam, you're doing a great job. But I think that's plenty of brushing. He won't have any hair left."

I stretched out the time it took to saddle Dandy, too. I moved the pad around, then the saddle, and fiddled with the buckle and strap.

The Harrises' group happened to be saddling up their horses across the ring from us. Of course, they were finished long before I was.

On his way outside Kevin Harris said to me, "Enough with the saddle!"

I liked it better when the Harrises were ignoring me.

"Mind your own business, Harris!" Peter said.

But once the Harrises and Sally were out of earshot, Maxine said, "Could you please hurry, Pam? We won't have any time left to ride."

So I buckled up the strap, once and for all.

We led our horses over to one of the outdoor riding rings. And I was finally forced to climb on.

Dandy stood quietly while Diana gave me a leg up. He even let me get settled in the saddle before he started shifting his feet around.

But I was so nervous about what he *might* do that I froze up totally.

"Pam, does your back hurt?" Diana asked. "You're sitting so stiffly today."

And Peter said, "You look like the statue of General Grant in Westbrook Park."

Even I had to giggle—I knew just what he meant.

But Jessie barely cracked a smile.

At lunch Maxine said, "Check out Lisa and Sally. They don't look very happy."

Lisa and Sally were sitting a few tables away from us. We couldn't hear what they were saying. But Lisa was flinging her hands around, and she had an angry expression on her face. Sally was shaking her head and shrugging a lot.

Suddenly Lisa jumped up from the table. She grabbed her lunch and marched away with it.

Sally just sat there for a moment, staring down at her sandwich. When she finally looked up, she caught Maxine, Jessie, Peter, and me staring at her.

Sally shook her head again, as if she were trying to clear it. Then she gave me a weak smile.

"Hmmph!" Jessie grunted. "Looks like you two are going to be great friends. And Lisa will be next!"

"Jessie!" I said sharply. "You have to be kidding."

But Jessie was already talking to Maxine about posting. She didn't answer me.

I couldn't understand why she was so upset. I mean, it was Lisa who had been nasty to Jessie, not Sally. But Jessie was lumping the two of them together as if they were the same person. Sally did have a mind of her own, didn't she?

That afternoon we had swimming. Jessie must have swum a hundred laps in the pool so that she wouldn't have to talk to me.

My dad was picking us up at four. But when we walked out of the barn, Mrs. Johnson's car was there, too.

"Jessie, why is your mom here?" I asked.

"I'm going to the dentist in Jamestown. Besides, I thought you might want to be alone with your *guest*," Jessie said, wrinkling her nose.

"Come on, Jessie!" I said. "That's the last thing I want!"

"Yeah. Well . . ." Jessie said, as if she knew better. She was starting to make me mad.

43

I thought she might walk away without another word.

But before she got into her car, Jessie turned back to me and said, "Hope it isn't too bad."

"Thanks," I said. And I felt a little better.

While I was watching Jessie's car drive away, Sally came out the side door of the barn. She was all alone. Then I saw Lisa and her brother leaving through the main door.

Sally stopped a few feet from me. "Hi," she said. She didn't even look at me—she looked down at the ground.

I didn't know how I should act, so I just said, "Hi. My dad is parked over there."

As we walked toward the car a minivan rolled past us and honked.

It was the Harrises. Lisa was in the front seat, staring straight ahead. Kevin made a face at us through a back window.

As soon as they were out of sight Sally suddenly became a lot friendlier. "It was nice of your mom to invite me to stay," she said. "And it was nice of you, too." She actually smiled, as though she meant it.

In the car Sally told me about Jamestown Elementary, where she would be a fifth grader in the fall. She asked about my school. She even talked to my dad.

As we pulled into our driveway Sally said, "Cool house."

She was excited to hear that it was over a hundred years old. She liked my room, too. And she especially liked Stanley.

"What an adorable cat!" Sally said, throwing herself across my bed to pet him.

Stanley is a big, fat, orange cat with cream-colored circles around his eyes that make him look a little like an owl.

"Thanks," I said. "Cats are my favorite animals."

"Yeah?" Sally said. "Mine too."

"Really? Not horses?" I asked, surprised.

Sally shook her head. "Horses are too big—they're kind of scary. In fact, I wouldn't be at Horizon Hills at all if it weren't for Lisa," she said.

I couldn't believe what I was hearing. Sally felt exactly the way I did about pony camp!

"Yeah, I know just what you mean," I said. "But Jessie can be pretty convincing. She wouldn't take no for an answer."

And that was all that I said about pony camp. Or about Jessie.

Cross my heart!

6

That night Sally didn't talk about Lisa at all. Well, she did say that she and Lisa had been best friends since first grade. But that was it.

We had shrimp curry for dinner. Sally said shrimp was her favorite food, just like it is mine. Afterward we watched a good movie on TV, about ghosts taking over a town. It was really spooky!

Of course, I wondered what Jessie was doing. But Sally and I had a good time. I have to admit, I sort of liked her. And I thought she liked me, too.

After all, we had a lot in common.

Just as the movie was ending, the phone rang. I grabbed it in the kitchen.

It was Jessie.

"Hi, how's it going?" she asked.

I knew Jessie wanted me to say it was awful. But it wasn't awful, and I didn't see why I should have to lie to my best friend.

So I said, "Fine."

"I get it! Sally can hear what you're saying, right?" Jessie guessed. "Or your mom is standing there?"

"No, it really is fine," I said. "When she's not with Lisa, Sally's—"

"So you don't need to talk to me," Jessie growled. "I shouldn't have bothered calling."

And she hung up the phone.

I could feel my face getting hot. Jessie was being impossible!

But I didn't mention it to Sally. When I went back to the den, she was digging in her tote bag. She took out a beaded bracelet she had made. It was really pretty, blue and silver, with a design of tiny purple hearts and arrows.

Sally had brought along some envelopes of colored beads. She showed me how to start a bracelet for myself.

By then it was time for bed.

Mom usually closes Stanley in the kitchen at night. Otherwise he wanders around the house poking into things and keeps everyone awake.

But Sally said, "Oh, Mrs. Werner, can't he sleep with us?"

So Stanley got to stay in my room. He curled up right on Sally's pillow. I guess Sally's allergic, because she sneezed a few times. But she didn't seem to mind.

Sometime that night I had my trail ride nightmare again. This time I was riding Dandy. He was running like the wind. His mane was streaming straight back, covering my eyes so that I couldn't see where we were going. When I pulled on the reins to stop him, he just ran faster!

I could hear Lisa laughing and Diana

49

shouting, "Pam! Relax!" Then I was losing my grip on the saddle. I was falling . . .

"Pam! Pam! Wake up!"

My eyes flew open. Sally was shaking me and Stanley was perched on my pillow, his tail brushing my face.

"Wow!" I mumbled, taking a deep breath.

"You were moaning and groaning! What was that all about?" Sally asked me.

I told Sally about the nightmare, and how I was terrified that Dandy would run away with me on the trail ride, and how I hadn't even told Jessie about it.

"I won't tell anybody, either," Sally said. "I promise."

Then we both went back to sleep.

The next morning neither of us mentioned my nightmare. I hoped Sally had forgotten all about it. After breakfast my mom drove us over to Jessie's house.

As soon as Jessie got into the car Sally clammed up. Jessie had nothing to say either.

Sally gazed out one side window, Jessie

the other. I sat in the middle and twiddled my thumbs. The ride to Horizon Hills seemed to last forever!

When we finally pulled up in front of the barn, I saw Lisa waiting for Sally outside.

Sally mumbled, "Thanks, Mrs. Werner," to my mom.

Then she scrambled out of the car like Jessie and I were both poison! She followed Lisa into the barn without a word.

And I thought Sally liked me? Wow, did I feel dumb!

Jessie and I looked at each other.

Jessie raised an eyebrow. "So you had a good time?" she asked.

"Yeah, can't you tell? Sally Keller and I are the best of friends," I said, rolling my eyes.

Jessie grinned. "Let's go check on Gracie," she said as we waved good-bye to Mom.

Thank goodness, Jessie and I were friends again!

G racie was glad to see us. But she was still hobbling around on three legs.

"Remember when I sprained my ankle last year?" Jessie asked. "It took me a month to get over it. With such a big swelling, Gracie will need at least a couple of weeks."

I must have looked unhappy, because Jessie patted my arm. "But you're doing great on Dandy," she said. "You'll have lots of fun with him on the trail ride."

Someone snickered.

Jessie and I looked up to find Lisa

Harris leaning against the stall door.

"Poor Dandy! Wasted on a major chicken!" Lisa said in a nasty tone.

"What is that supposed to mean?" Jessie said. "Pam is not a chicken!"

I could see Sally over Lisa's shoulder. But as soon as I caught her eye, Sally looked away.

"Oh, yeah? That shows what you know!" said Lisa. "She doesn't deserve Dandy. She's scared to death of horses. And she hates it here. She wouldn't even be at pony camp if you weren't so pushy. *You* forced her to come!"

"Says who?" Jessie asked angrily.

"Says her!" said Lisa, pointing at me. "She told Sally last night. Just ask her!"

"Well, Pam?" said Jessie, her eyes narrowed as she looked at me.

"Jessie, I didn't say that!" I yelped. "All I said was that I—"

"Thanks a lot!" Jessie cried. "Feel free to stop coming here anytime!"

Jessie stamped away.

"So now you can leave pony camp, and *I* can ride Dandy!" said Lisa. She gave me a satisfied smirk.

Sally wouldn't look at me. She was staring into space, as if she didn't even hear what was going on.

"Do you know why Kathy Farrow wanted to sell Dandy?" Lisa asked.

"Yes. Because her legs are too long for him," I replied.

"No. Because Dandy is a runaway," Lisa said with a giggle. "Better watch out on the trail ride. You could end up in California!"

Then they left me standing alone in Gracie's stall, wishing I had never heard of Sally Keller, Lisa Harris, or Horizon Hills!

I closed Gracie's door and walked slowly up the alley to Dandy's stall.

Dandy nudged at my hand, like Gracie does. Since I had forgotten to give Gracie her apple slices, I fed them to Dandy instead. When he finished eating them, he bumped his head on my arm, as if he wanted to be my friend.

I rubbed his nose and sniffled a little. I was glad Dandy was being nice to me. I needed all the friends I could get.

That morning I focused on posting: "Aah-one, aah-two, aah-one . . ."

"Excellent, Pam!" Diana called out. "You and Dandy are getting along great!"

But Jessie and I weren't.

After we ride, the four of us usually meet at the lockers next to Mr. Morgan's office. That's where we keep our riding hats when we're not using them, and our bathing suits, and our lunches. And that's where I thought Jessie and I would be able to talk.

But that day Jessie unsaddled Ranger in about a minute flat. She practically dragged him up the alley to his stall. Then she dashed toward the lockers.

Jessie raced out the side door, past Maxine, Peter, and me, before we had even picked up our lunches.

"What's going on?" Maxine asked me. "Is something wrong between you and Jessie?"

"Jessie's upset about Sally spending the night at my house," I told Maxine. "And about some things that Lisa said."

"Girl stuff!" Peter sighed. "Got any corn chips?"

Maxine just said, "Lisa loves to cause trouble."

Lisa had caused plenty this time!

When Maxine, Peter, and I got outside, Jessie was sitting by herself at one end of a table. The other end was taken by a couple of intermediate girls. There was no room for us.

We played baseball that afternoon, and Jessie and I were on opposite teams. We couldn't have spoken if we had wanted to.

But I thought we could talk on the way home. Jessie would be trapped with me in the backseat of the car. I could explain to her about my dream and everything.

But it didn't work that way.

Mr. Johnson was picking us up. Jessie stormed out of the barn ahead of me to climb into the front seat beside her father. She flipped on the radio and started singing along.

That left me in the backseat with no best friend.

8

The last time Jessie and I had a fight was in first grade. Jessie told me that our teacher, Mrs. Donally, wouldn't mind if we climbed onto the roof of the sports shed. And that I was a wimp if I didn't do it.

But Mrs. Donally *did* mind, plenty! Jessie and I both got into big trouble.

I got mad at Jessie. We didn't speak for a few days. And then she said she was sorry, and we were friends again.

But this time around it was partly my fault. I should have told Jessie I was afraid right from the start.

Jessie is much more stubborn than I am. She might not speak to me for *years*!

Maxine wanted to help. On Friday morning she tried to talk to Jessie herself.

"Jessie," Maxine said, "Pam is really upset that—"

"If she's so upset, she should tell her friend Sally Keller about it!" Jessie interrupted. "I'm too bossy for Pam anyway." Then she stormed off to Ranger's stall.

Maxine looked at me and shrugged. "Jessie's feelings are hurt. Maybe you should leave her alone until she cools off."

"I don't think I have any choice," I said sadly.

All day I could tell that Lisa was talking about me. She kept looking over at me and whispering to Sally. Then she would giggle behind her hand. And every time she was close enough to me, she would whisper, "Runaway!"

But now I was certain about one thing. Lisa was *not* going to get Dandy—not even if he turned the trail ride into the Kentucky Derby!

Before we went home that afternoon, I looked for Diana in the barn. She was grooming her own horse, Conan.

"Diana, can I talk to you for a second?" I said over the stall door.

"Hi, Pam," Diana said. "Sure! Want to help me out at the same time?"

She handed me a brush under Conan's stomach. "You brush that side, and I'll do this one," Diana said.

I had never been near such a humongous animal, besides the elephants at the zoo! Conan is so tall that Diana practically needs a ladder to get on him.

"What's up?" Diana asked.

I started to brush. "There's something I have to tell you," I said. I took a deep breath before I went on. "Horses are too big, and they move too fast, and I never know what they're thinking. They scare me!"

"What?" Diana stopped brushing and ducked under Conan's neck to stare at me. "Pam, you've been doing awfully well with

61

your riding for someone who's afraid of horses."

"That's because of Gracie," I said quickly. "I'm not afraid of her."

"You're riding Dandy well, too," Diana said.

"But I don't feel right about him. I feel—" I began.

Before I could finish, Diana broke in. "And let me just point out that you're standing about six inches away from a horse the size of a moose. You don't seem ready to keel over from terror!"

I glanced up at Conan's big brown eye. It was watching me with interest. But it didn't look scary.

I cleared my throat. "Diana, Lisa Harris says Dandy is a runaway. She says that's why the Farrows sold him."

"Lisa Harris!" Diana raised her eyebrows. "She really is too much! Pam, do you believe Mr. Morgan would stick a camper on a runaway horse?"

"I guess not," I said. It did sound kind

of silly when she put it that way.

"Do you know what I think?" Diana asked. "I think that little by little, without you really noticing it, you're getting over being afraid of horses."

Could that be true? I had never thought about it like that.

"The more you understand horses, the less scary they'll seem," Diana said. "I'll be here at the stable tomorrow afternoon. Why don't you stop by between one and four?"

"That's exactly what I wanted to ask you!" I said. "If you could give me a private lesson before the trail ride."

"It won't be a lesson," Diana said, starting to brush Conan again. "Let's call it a get-together."

And I saw what she meant when I got there on Saturday afternoon.

"No riding today," Diana told me as I started toward Dandy's stall. "We'll just walk around and talk to some of the horses."

As we headed up the alley Diana said,

"You told me that you never know what horses are thinking. I'm going to show you some ways to figure that out."

We stopped outside Conan's stall. He was dozing in a corner when Diana quietly opened the stall door.

"Ears are important," Diana said in a low voice. "When horses are sleeping or just very relaxed, their ears hang loose and to the sides."

Conan's ears were doing exactly that, until he heard Diana's voice. Then he woke up and raised his head. His ears pricked up and pointed forward, in our direction.

"That means he's interested and paying close attention," Diana said. "When you're riding a horse, you can tell if he's alert by watching his ears. Interested ears move forward and backward—the horse is looking ahead and listening to you at the same time."

"Dandy does that!" I said.

"Right," said Diana. "He can't see behind him. But he wants to know what you're up to, as much as you want to know about him. So he uses his ears."

I gave Conan a pat before we left his stall.

"Now I'll show you ears to be careful around," Diana said.

We stopped in front of another stall. A sign on the door said BEWARE.

I expected a real monster of a horse inside. But when Diana pushed the door open, I saw a Shetland pony about the size of a big dog!

I started to laugh. "Beware of *him*?" I said.

"You'd better believe it!" said Diana. "Size has nothing to do with temper. Conan would never hurt you. But Sam here might try. See his ears?"

Sam took a hard look at us and pressed his ears straight back, flat against his neck! I had never seen Dandy's ears do that.

"That's a bad sign," Diana said. "A horse with his ears flat back is getting angry. Sam might bite or kick. If you were riding him, he might try to throw you off."

"Who has to ride him?" I asked. Whoever it was, I felt sorry for them.

"No one," Diana told me. "Sam is very old and very cranky!"

We backed carefully out of the stall. Diana closed the stall door and latched it.

I peered over the closed door. Sam's ears had loosened up—they were hanging out to the sides now.

"He's about to take a nap?" I guessed.

"You got it!" said Diana. "Let's go outside for a minute or two. Some of the horses have been turned into the field.

"Horses are herd animals—in the wild, they live in large groups. They have to be able to let each other know what they are thinking," Diana explained on our way to the field. "Misunderstandings lead to fights."

"Tell me about it!" I muttered. Maybe if people had long ears like horses, there were would be fewer problems.

Diana and I watched the horses as they played. After we checked out their ears, Diana explained what it meant when they held their tails in different ways.

By the time we were done, I was pretty good at reading horse sign language!

9

As far as I could tell, Dandy's signals were all the right kind.

But Jessie's weren't.

She didn't call me over the weekend. And when she and her mom picked me up on Monday, she barely nodded hello.

That morning at Horizon Hills, she stayed away from me as much as she could. But I did get one small smile out of her.

After we finished riding in the outdoor ring, I led Dandy toward the barn. Lisa dragged Rambo up beside us to say, "Looking forward to a runaway trail ride?

There's still time to switch horses, you know."

I pulled Dandy to a stop and glared at her.

If I had been a horse, my ears would have been plastered back to my neck! My tail would have been swishing a mile a minute!

As it was I shouted, "I am sick of you causing trouble, Lisa Harris! Get out of my face!"

Peter was right behind me. "Way to go, Pam!" he yelled.

"Well, excuse me!" Lisa said. "I was just trying to warn you."

"I don't need your help!" I told her.

Jessie and Ranger kept walking toward the barn. But I saw Jessie's mouth curl up in a tiny smile.

At lunchtime I grabbed my sandwich from the lockers before anybody else.

"Hey, Pam, where are you going in such a hurry?" Peter called down the alley.

"Out back," I said. "See you later."

I stopped by Gracie's stall on my way—to

say hello and feed her a peppermint stick.

I thought her leg looked a little bit better. She was resting the tip of her back hoof on the ground instead of holding it up in the air.

But I knew I would be with Dandy on the trail ride the next day. And I wanted to get a look at the field we would be riding through.

When I went through the back door of the barn, I stopped in surprise. It was beautiful out there! The clumps of grass were dark green and knee-high, with little yellow and white flowers scattered around. A breeze was blowing. If I took a deep breath, I could smell the ocean.

I was sitting on a stump, eating my tuna sandwich, when somebody said, "Hey."

It was Jessie!

"Hi," I said.

"What are you doing out here?" she asked.

"Imagining tomorrow," I told her.

Jessie stared up at the sky for a minute. Then she said, "Pam, why didn't you tell me you hated Horizon Hills? We're best friends, but I didn't even know you were unhappy until Lisa told me!"

"I never hated it, Jessie. I was afraid of horses," I said. "And the truth is, I *wouldn't* have come here if it wasn't for you."

Jessie sighed. "Yeah, I know," she said. "I'm pushy, and bossy, and—"

"And you make me do things that turn out to be fun!" I told her.

"Fun?" Jessie said, surprised.

"Fun!" I said. "I'm not afraid anymore."

Jessie's face broke into a grin. "Really?"

I nodded. "I'm starting to think horses are cool—even Dandy," I said.

"All right!" Jessie exclaimed.

I looked out at the field again. "I'm still a little worried about the trail ride, though. I had this horrible dream about a horse running away with me."

"No problem," Jessie said. "Maxine and I

will ride in front of you. If Dandy even thinks about running away, he'll have to climb over us first."

She stuck out her hand. "Friends again?" she asked.

I shook it, hard. "Forever," I said.

I woke up the next morning with butter-flies in my stomach. It was the day of the trail ride!

Mom and I drove to Jessie's house. Jessie was waiting on her front steps. She was holding a couple of small plastic bags.

"Hi, Mrs. Werner," Jessie said, climbing into the backseat next to me.

She handed me one of the plastic bags. It was full of raisins, almonds, sunflower seeds, and other good stuff.

"Trail mix," Jessie said. "For the trail ride. Personally mixed by me."

"Thanks," I said. It was like we had never had a fight.

10

A t the barn it seemed like every single horse was being saddled.

"It's because all the instructors are going to ride, too," Maxine told us.

"And Mr. Morgan," said Peter. "He was putting a bridle on a big chestnut."

Peter had something else on his mind. "If Mr. Morgan is riding along with us," he said, "I wonder who's bringing the food for the cookout."

"Mrs. Morgan," Diana told him, tightening the strap around Conan's stomach. "I saw her loading the van with mounds of hot dogs

and hamburgers and huge bags of groceries."

Diana told us that we would be riding single file, in a long line. Mr. Morgan would lead us on the big chestnut. And an instructor would ride at the end of each group of campers.

"Pam, you can go first in our group," Diana said. But Jessie quickly shook her head.

"No, I'll go first, and then Maxine," she said.

Diana shrugged. "Okay. Then Pam, and Peter, and I'll bring up the rear."

So I was covered in front and in back. I was actually excited for the trail ride to start!

The line was forming in the field. We led our horses over, and Diana helped us get mounted.

That's when I noticed the group ahead of us. They were intermediates—and not just any intermediates: Lisa and Kevin Harris, Sally Keller, and Bill Frano.

Maxine backed her horse up to me and said, "Don't worry about them. Their instructor, Donald Metz, is tough. He doesn't let the Harrises get away with anything."

Kevin had his eye on Peter. I could tell he was about to open his mouth to make a nasty remark.

But Donald Metz barked, "Kevin, pay attention to what *you're* doing! Straighten up your feet! Look intermediate!"

Kevin turned bright red, and Peter and Jessie giggled.

It didn't stop Lisa from trying to scare me, though. She caught my eye and nodded wisely.

I knew what she meant. She was reminding me that Dandy was a runaway.

But Dandy's little ears were flicking back and forth as he took everything in. His tail was hanging loose. He was quiet, relaxed, and interested.

And I knew Lisa was wrong about him.

Now everybody was mounted. Mr. Morgan rode up and down the line, just to make sure all the saddles were strapped on tightly and all the riders were wearing their hats.

Then he trotted back to the front of the line.

"Are we ready?" he called out.

"Ready!" we called back.

Mr. Morgan stuck his hand up into the air and waved it forward. "We're on our way!" he said.

The line of horses and riders headed across the wide field at a slow trot. It looked so cool.

"We're like the pioneers!" Jessie exclaimed from in front of me. "On our way west!"

That was exactly what I had been thinking. Jessie turned a little in her saddle, and we grinned at each other.

When we got to the far side of the field, we rode into the woods. There were evergreens, oaks, and maples. A narrow trail wound through them, dark green and shady.

We slowed to a walk, which gave us time

to look at all the trees. I saw a ton of butter-flies and some rabbits. Diana even pointed out a deer, hiding behind a clump of blue-berry bushes!

There were so many things to look at that I didn't worry about Dandy at all.

But there was a tense moment at the side of a stream. Since it had rained the night before, the stream was running pretty quickly.

Maybe Dandy was scared of the gurgling noises the water was making. Anyway, he walked up to the stream bank easily enough. But as soon as he got a good look at the water, his ears pointed straight ahead and he snorted. Then he stopped short!

Since I wasn't ready for it, I fell forward. I grabbed Dandy's neck and hung on. My rid-ing hat fell off and landed on the ground with a thud.

Dandy backed up pretty fast.

But Diana was off Conan. She grabbed our bridle in a split second.

I could hear giggling. It was probably Lisa, somewhere ahead of us.

But I knew this wasn't Dandy's fault. He was frightened. I scrambled back into the saddle. Diana gave me my hat back and made sure I buckled it tight.

Then Jessie was beside me. "Good save," she said.

"I learned it from you," I told her. "Maybe if you and Ranger get on one side of me and Maxine goes on the other side, Dandy won't be afraid anymore."

"Great idea," Diana agreed.

Knee to knee, Jessie, Maxine, and I walked our horses slowly back to the stream in a tight row. We stood there for a second, letting Dandy look at the water.

I could tell that Dandy felt safer. Our three horses went across in step, like a drill team!

As soon as we got to the far side of the stream Dandy's ears started twitching happily back and forth again.

Lisa's group had moved ahead while we were stopped at the stream. Now another beginners group was in front of us. So we didn't have to listen to Lisa or Kevin—or look at Sally—for the rest of the ride.

11

It took almost an hour for everyone to wind through the trees. Then the sand dunes began. That was fun, because the horses had to kind of hop up the dunes while we hung on tight with our legs. And getting down the dunes was sort of like sledding—if you can imagine going sledding on a horse!

"This reminds me of a roller coaster at an amusement park," Jessie said as we started up another dune.

"I-I-I w-w-wish I h-h-h-had an amusement p-p-park h-h-h-hot dog," said Peter as he bumped along behind me.

As soon as the dunes smoothed out Jessie and I shared our trail mix with him. And with Maxine and Diana.

Finally we could see the ocean shining in the distance!

"We'll trot!" Mr. Morgan called out. "But stay in line."

Dandy couldn't have been better behaved. Head bobbing up and down, ears pointing forward and then back, he trotted along smoothly. I even posted!

"Hey, the real thing!" Jessie called to me. "Outdoor posting!"

"I think *we* look intermediate!" said Maxine.

When we got to the beach, Mrs. Morgan's van was waiting, along with a couple of trucks driven by stablehands. One truck had a rubber water trough in the back for the horses to drink out of. The other was full of volleyball nets and barbecue grills and floats for swimming.

We had all worn our bathing suits under our riding clothes. As soon as we had loosened the saddles and watered our horses, we turned them over to the stable-hands.

Then we peeled down to our bathing suits and dived into the ocean. The cool water felt fantastic!

We swam for a while. Then the instructors organized a couple of volleyball games on the beach. Sally and I ended up on the same team.

After a few minutes she edged over to talk to me.

"Listen, Pam," Sally said in a low voice, "I'm sorry if I did anything to make problems between you and Jessie."

The only right answer would have been, "Why did you open your big mouth, then?" But I didn't say anything.

Sally went on, "But when Lisa asked me what you were like, I had to tell her something!"

"And that was all you could come up with?" I asked.

"You know how Lisa is," Sally murmured.

Suddenly Lisa called out sharply from the other side of the net, "Sally, where are you?"

Sally jumped away from me like she had stepped on hot coals. But she whispered over her shoulder, "Anyway, sorry."

Sally isn't so bad by herself. But she's totally under Lisa's thumb.

"I did get one good thing out of the sleepover with Sally," I told Jessie when the game was over.

"What?" Jessie asked, frowning a little.

"Sally taught me how to make dynamite beaded bracelets," I said.

"Cool!" Jessie said, brightening. "Let's make huge matching ones and wear them to Horizon Hills, just to get Sally and Lisa crazy!"

I thought it was a great idea.

After we ate lunch, there was a sand castle contest. Then we swam a little bit more.

And then it was time to dry off, pull on our riding clothes, and head back to Horizon Hills.

The ride back was quieter. The kids were tired from the riding and swimming and volleyball games. And the horses knew where they were going now, so they were relaxed.

Dandy didn't even slow down at the stream—he marched straight across.

But we hadn't ridden very far past the water when we heard shouts from behind us.

"No! Rambo! What are you *doing*?" a girl screeched.

"That sounds like Lisa!" said Jessie.

We pulled our horses to a stop and looked back toward the stream.

Rambo, with Lisa aboard, was standing in the center of the stream. Lisa was kicking his sides, but he didn't budge.

Rambo's ears were pricked up and forward. "His ears aren't plastered back, so he isn't mad," I said. "I wonder what he's doing."

"He's really getting into it!" Jessie said, giggling.

Rambo had lifted a front leg up high. He was pawing the water! He was splashing it everywhere!

"Diana, what *is* he doing?" Maxine asked.

Diana was grinning. "Playing. Usually the next step is—"

Donald Metz jumped off his horse and into the stream to grab Rambo's bridle.

"He's going to drag Rambo and Lisa out," Jessie said. "Too bad—just when things were getting interesting."

But it didn't work. Rambo bent his front legs and his front end dropped down.

"He looks like a camel!" Peter said.

In slow motion Rambo lowered himself into the water. Donald Metz pulled Lisa out of the way just before Rambo lay down on his side in the stream, saddle and all!

"I'm all wet!" Lisa was screeching. She was standing in the stream, the water almost to her knees. "My boots are ruined!"

I would have liked to see more.

But Diana said, "We'd better move along, group. We're holding up the line."

My last view of Lisa was of her hunched over on the stream bank, pouring water out of one of her boots.

"You couldn't call Rambo a runaway," I said to Jessie. "But you could definitely call him a *swimaway*!"

Jessie laughed. And then my best friend and I trotted our horses through the woods, across the field, and back to the barn. It was the best trail ride ever!